Sue Raymond

Window Pane

By Sue Raymond

Sue Raymond

Publisher: Upon Eagle's Wings, Malachi Ink

516 East Park Avenue, Des Moines, IA 50315

Cover Art:

Matt Davenport, Davenport Writes LLC

Editor: Michele Charron

Sue Raymond

DEDICATION

I wish to thank everyone that cheered me on throughout the publishing process of this novella. I also wish to give credit to the Lord for His mercy and love. He is my strength and my shield. Without the Lord, nothing is possible.

CONTENTS

ACKNOWLEDGMENTS

I wish to acknowledge my writing team Davenport Writes, LLC, which is essential to the publication of my novels. And a heartfelt thank you to our departed team member, Dan.

CHAPTER 1

The rain streaked the window pane against the pitch black night. Thunder rumbled far away; it echoed the emptiness she felt within her soul. Where was she? Why did they leave her here? She stared at the image reflected in the window. Who was this strange woman staring back at her? She had no recollection of how she got here, who brought her here or why. The image distorted in the waves of rain running down the window.

The harder she tried to understand what was going on the more frustration swelled within her soul. How could the old crone's reflection in the window be her? She raised her fist to smash the image and stopped in horror. The fist was age speckled and the skin hung loose on the bony fingers. She twirled around to flee this horrible nightmare but her body creaked and groaned in protest. Nothing she saw was familiar. The furniture in the small room was pleasant enough, but held no comfort. The walls were painted in pale beige. The pictures on the walls beckoned to her, yet the people were not identifiable. Where were the matching pair of wingback chairs she cuddled up in under the soft quilt watching the flames flicker in the fireplace?

She hobbled to the door. Hospital stench bombarded her senses as she pulled the heavy door open. The lights were very dim in the narrow hallway, making it nearly impossible for her to see where she was going. She held her shaky hand out in front of her as she shuffled her feet to keep her footsteps as quiet as she could. If only she could get out of wherever this was, maybe she could find her way home.

She passed door after door, hearing low moans along with whiffs of obnoxious odors coming from behind the doors. She finally reached the end of the hall. It emptied out into a larger corridor that had seven other hallways branching off just like the one where she stood.

In the middle of the corridor was a central desk. The only light in the corridor was a dim light from a computer screen sitting on the desk. On the other side of the desk above a double set of doors blinked a neon red exit sign.

She crept towards the doors. The exit sign beckoned to her to hurry as there was not much time for her to escape to freedom. The nearer she came the harder it was to breathe. Her heartbeat started pounding in her ears. Her legs were trembling by the time she arrived at the door. She leaned against the door, closing her eyes. The cool wood felt good to her feverish cheek. She drew a breath deep as she could muster before she tried to stand straight. Tiny shards of colored lights danced in front of her eyes as she grabbed the lever door handle. She shoved it down with all her weight.

She heard a click as the door latch came free. A second later, a loud alarm sounded. She pushed the door as hard as she could, trying to squeeze by the heavy door. Rain splashed against her face as she wedged her body in the small opening.

Heavy footsteps rumbled above the sound of the

rain as she felt the door move outward. Just as she freed herself, a firm gentle hand caught her by the arm and pulled her back.

"Hey, what do you think you are doing trying to go out in this rain storm?" The large orderly swept her up in his arms and pulled the door shut. He set her in the wheelchair that was by the desk, and then reached over the desk, shutting off the alarm. He knelt by the chair, placed his mammoth hand over the fragile shoulder. "You know I cannot allow you out this late at night in the midst of a downpour. Let's get you back in your room and in dry clothes. I may even be able to find a little bit of cocoa to warm you from the chill." His eyes sparkled with kindness as he gently lifted her feet up on the wheelchair footrest.

The wheelchair squeaked as the small front wheels wobbled severely. He had a hard time keeping the chair going in a straight line. "Looks like I'm going to have to get the oil can out again." He gave a sigh as he bumped the door to her room open with his foot and backed into the room. He wheeled her over by the bed then went and got a towel, draping it over her shoulders. He then got a gown out of the dresser, laying it on the bed. "Here is a nice warm gown for you to change into while I finish making my rounds, then I will get you a cup of cocoa."He lifted her out of the wheel chair and sat her on the bed.

He folded the wheelchair as he gave her a warm smile, then he was gone. She looked down at the gown and then over at the rain streaked window. Even though he was nice, she did not want their cocoa. It always had a bitter after taste. It made her groggy and she could not think straight for hours afterwards. She changed and threw the wet gown in the hamper.

The door across the room opened, admitting a tall, elegant, mature man carrying a covered tray. He smiled at her as he set the tray on the small table. "Figured the storm would wake you, here, sit down. I made you a nice cup of French vanilla mocha cocoa. I even swiped extra marshmallows for us." He gently guided her to the chaise before sitting beside her, removing the cover, revealing an array of delicious petit fours with two steaming mugs of cocoa. "Thunder always upset you."

She kept an eye on his every movement as he prepared the mug of cocoa with marshmallows for her. His mannerisms and twinkling gray eyes gave her a small comfort in this sterile environment. The gray hair over his ears added to his charm as the laugh lines crinkled at the edges of his eyes.

He held out the mug toward her. The delicious aroma won her over and she carefully took it wrapping her thin fingers around the mug. Its warmth spread through her fingers up her slender wrists traveling to her heart. There, it slowly wiped away the hollowness and filled her with hope. She watched as he sat back and sipped his cocoa and popped a petit four in his mouth. He closed his eyes as he chewed. A satisfied grin spread across his face.

She sat there, sipping from the mug, as she kept a cautious eye on the man's movements. There was something strange about how he knew she would like this cocoa. It was as if he could reach into her mind and pull out things prohibited to her. She wanted to throw the mug against the wall and scream questions at him.

He sat up and handed her a petit four before snatching several more and popped them into his cheeks. He looked like a chipmunk gathering nuts for the winter. He turned and tried to smile at her. The chocolate covered teeth and crooked grin broke down her resistance and she gave a small giggle.

He washed the petit four down before joining her in the giggle. "I love to hear you laugh. It lightens your soul and heart when you do."

She sat the cup and petit four down. "Do I know you? I cannot remember anything anymore. I do not know where I am or how I got here. Please help me." A tear gathered in the corner of her eye.

He set the cup down and reached into his pocket withdrawing a large embroidered monogrammed handkerchief and dried the tear. He handed her the handkerchief as he gently pulled her to her feet and into his embrace. There she felt comfort, peace, and fulfillment.

He caressed her hair as he leaned his chin on the top of her head.

CHAPTER 2

She woke in the bed with the sun beams streaming in the window. She did not know how she got into bed or when the elegant man had disappeared. There was a sharp rap on the door. A second later a stout nurse with a stony face came barging into the room.

"There you are! What are you doing still in bed? Breakfast is almost over. I suppose you had a hard night again because of the rain. Well let's get you dressed and see if there is anything left for you to eat for breakfast." The nurse turned to the dresser to pull clothes out.

She slowly pulled back the cover, saddened that she must have dreamed the whole thing last night, the gentle orderly, the elegant elderly man, and the delicious cocoa. Her eyes widened as she discovered the handkerchief corner sticking out from under her pillow. She quickly slid the corner under the pillow right before the nurse turned back toward her.

"Okay this should keep you warm enough. Let's get you ready for the day."

Fifteen minutes later, she was ready. As nurse turned to place the gown in the hamper, she slipped the handkerchief from its hiding place and in the sleeve of her sweater. Once there, she felt better. The heaviness was not quite so burdensome. The handkerchief proved that she did not dream them up. They were real. Someone knew her. Someone cared.

The nurse turned and helped her to her feet. They slowly left the room and walked down the narrow hallway to the main corridor. Folding chairs and tables had been haphazardly been set up. There were a variety of elderly people sitting at the tables trying to down the unpalatable gray mush sitting in front of them. The nurse directed her to an empty chair then left to get her breakfast.

She sat down and glanced around at her table companions. Each had a vacant stare in their eyes as they shoveled spoonful after spoonful of gray mush in their mouths. They barely swallowed before another spoonful followed the last. She gave a silent shudder as she watched.

The nurse returned and set several pieces of toast in front of her. "This was all that was left. If it dries up enough, everyone will be able to go out in the garden for some fresh air. So hurry up and eat." She walked away without looking back.

She started to reach for a piece of toast when a hand whipped out from the person next to her and snatched the toast from her plate. The person broke the toast in pieces, giving them to the others at the table. They gobbled the pieces down, then went back and slowly shoveled the rest of the mush in their mouths.

She gave a sigh and a small smile at the poor souls before she rose and went over to the window watching the last of the rain drops run down the window and out of sight.

CHAPTER 3

The rest of the day she spent at the corridor window watching the birds flutter in the bird bath. They also pecked at the ground for insects that the rain washed out of their hiding place and onto the cement patio. She fingered the handkerchief in her sleeve wondering if she would ever see him again. The handkerchief was real so it proved the rest was also, right?

Doubt set in the longer she watched the other residents mill around aimlessly up and down the halls, since the nurse decided it was too wet to go outside. She glanced up time to time to see where the nurse was. The nurse did not move from the center desk and kept an ever watchful eye on the front door. It never seemed to be unguarded.

She gave up and slowly went back to her room. She went over to the pictures on the wall and tried to remember who or where the pictures were taken. The center picture was the most familiar to her. It was a picture of a young girl at the blossom of womanhood. Her eyes shined with a glow coming from deep within her soul. It poured forth, bathing her in a loveliness that only could come from being in love. She was blowing bubbles at the person behind the camera.

She gave a sigh as nothing came to her mind on who this young girl was. Another picture showed the same girl several years older, holding a baby in her arms. She had the baby's hand in hers as they waved at the unseen photographer behind the lens. At this point she lost interest in the rest of the picture.

She heard the distant roll of thunder. It was going to rain again. She shuddered at the thought. Why did the rain bother her so much? For some reason she felt at one time the rain brought comfort. But now it only filled her with dread, deep, dark, forbidding dread.

She drew the light knitted shawl from the stiff chair and wrapped it around her. The sound of light rain splattering against the window drew her to it. She tried to resist but the pull was too strong and she found herself leaning her forehead against the ice cold pane. Tears matched the raindrops running down the window pane. Where were they? She had searched all through the halls for any trace of them. She had even broke down and asked the staff about them. The answers she received plunged her in despair. Everyone confirmed each other's answer. There was no one matching their description on staff.

How could they not be real? The handkerchief is real and he gave it to her so he had to be real. The orderly carried her to the wheelchair when she felt so faint. She felt their touch, their scent traveled throughout her psyche, raising her spirit. The nurse wanted to give her a sedative so she stopped asking. All too soon, her spirit was despondent once again and she felt lost and alone.

Time ticked by as the rain raged outside. Her eyes were swollen from the tears. She heard the bell for bedtime. She knew the nurse would be looking in to make sure that she was complying with the rules. She heard the door close two doors down and the sturdy footsteps heading her way. She hurried as fast as she could to the bed and slid under the covers. She shut off the lamp on the nightstand as the door next door shut with the footsteps echoing off the walls closing in on her. She closed her eyes just as the door opened and a flashlight beam fell across her face for a second, and then darted away to the next room.

She waited until she heard the footsteps come back and diminish down the hall before she cautiously crawled out of bed and went back to the window. The lightning started flashing in the distance. She watched as it arced in a jagged streak, ripping the blackened sky in two for a split second, and then plunged the sky back into liquid inky blackness as it disappeared. The lightning grew in intenseness coming closer with each strike.

The lightning struck out on the patio lighting up the area. She was stunned for a second then she saw her. The rain diffused her shape slightly then she was gone back into the dark. She searched the darkness for any sign of her. Why would anyone be out in this downpour? The lightning cracked across the sky illuminating the area once more. She saw her dancing and swirling in the puddles as she kicked up large sprays of water. Her Byzantium lace dress quickly darkened to the color of eggplant in the soaking rain. Her face showed her spirit was still flying high, dancing among the raindrops. She watched pressing her hand firmly against the window pane as the young girl swirled closer to the window. She could almost make out her features in the next flash of lightning. Her hair was plastered against her head showing off her heart shape face and beautiful smile. The girl swirled away from the window, dancing and swaying to the sound of the thunder. Then all she could see was darkness.

She couldn't believe her eyes. Was the girl real or was she another illusion like the men last night? She could have watched her dance all night. She wished that she was out there with her dancing in the rain, allowing the rain to wash way all the cares burdening her soul. She stood there in hopes the girl would come back.

She pulled herself away from the window. She walked back to the chair and laid the shawl on the back of the chair. She made her way to the dresser and changed to her gown. She crawled into bed and closed her eyes as her mind replayed the girl's dance over and over. The rain lost some of it dreadful hold on her soul as she fell asleep dreaming of the dancing girl in the rain.

CHAPTER 4

She woke to the sound of distant thunder. It seemed that the rain would never give up. She could still feel the dance's effect on her soul. The aches in her body were not as painful as yesterday. She dressed and hid the handkerchief under the pillow on the chaise, then made her way down to the center hallway. As she approached the end of the hall she reasoned that there should be a record of who she was at the center desk. If she could only get a look at her file it would clear everything up, then she could make sense of this nightmare.

She peered around the corner watching the nurse who was at the computer. There was a crash in the kitchen with loud swearing. The nurse abandoned her post to see what the trouble was this time. She waited until the nurse disappeared through the kitchen door before she made her way over to the desk and found the file cabinet. She tried to pull the drawer open. It gave a loud groan in protest before it opened. She rifled through the files until she came to the room assignments. She ran her finger down the list until she came to her room number. She looked in disbelief. According to the list her room was unoccupied.

She slid the file back in the cabinet and pushed with all her might but the drawer would not close completely. She tried to reopen it to see if it was off kilter but it would not move either way. She heard the nurse telling the cook to be more careful next time as the kitchen door started to open.

She hurried back to the hallway as fast as her ancient legs would carry her. She slid around the corner just at the nurse walked out of the kitchen. Her heart was hammering in her chest and she felt faint. She could hardly draw a breath. She held on to the metal railing attached to the wall. She closed her eyes willing her heart to slow down so she could escape before being discovered by the nurse. She felt another presence standing in front of her. She slowly opened her eyes staring at the black and white tiled floor. She expected to see the stout nurse's white nursing shoes. A large black pair of men's shoe greeted her. She looked up at the gentle smiling face of the orderly from the other night. She tried to say something, however, no sound but a small gasp escaped her throat.

He put a finger to his lips as he glanced around the corner at the desk. The nurse was fighting with the drawer mumbling that whoever was messing in the files would regret their transgression most certainly. He looked down at her, "Let's get you out of the hall so the nurse does not catch us." He swept her up in his strong arms and swiftly walked back to her room. She leaned her head on his chest listening to his strong steady heartbeat. It calmed her and eased the pain in her chest. She drew in a cleansing breath as they entered her room. He set her on the chaise, placing the couch pillow under her feet.

She watched him acutely trying to place why he

was so familiar to her and why she felt so comfortable with him. He drew the curtain back and watched the rain run down the window pane.

"Is she out there? Did she come back?"

He turned, "Who are you asking about, sweetie?"

"The young girl in the Byzantium lace dress, she was dancing in the rain last night. It was delightful to watch her dance so carefree, kicking the water up."

He smiled looking out the window again, "No she isn't here."

"Why doesn't anyone on the staff know you? I asked everyone I could and no one knew anything about you or the elderly gentleman that brought me that delicious cocoa." She tried to sit up.

He moved from the window and knelt beside the chaise, laying a gentle hand on her shoulder. His smile eased the stress raging in her soul. "I am only here to help a very select few people. Most of the staff is too wrapped up in their own universe to see past their nose. Just know I will be here for you whenever you need me. I need you to not over stress your body right now. Everything will become clear in just a little while. You will have to be patient. It will not be much longer, I promise. Everything is being prepared for you then you will have the freedom you are craving." He rose and walked over to the door. "Remember, rest for a while then take it easy while you wait." He smiled at her then left.

She leaned back on the pillow, closed her eyes and allowed the memory of the girl dancing in the storm to play over and over until she fell asleep.

CHAPTER 5

She woke to the roaring thunder. Flashes of lightning struck seconds later after the thunder then it thundered from the latest flash of lightning. She turned the lamp on then rose and looked out of the window. She wondered if the girl would come and dance for her again.

Soon she tired of watching the rain run down the window pane. She turned away and walked over to the pictures. As she stared at them she noticed a small detail in one of the pictures. The young woman had a toddler on her lap. They were embroidering a handkerchief. Broad smiles caressed their faces revealing the joy bubbling up in their souls.

She pulled the handkerchief free from the hiding place under the pillow. She held it up to the picture. They had the design halfway done. She gave a small gasp.

They were embroidering the handkerchief she held in her hand.

She suddenly felt very weak and sat down on the edge of the bed. Who were these people and how did they fit in this puzzle? The more she tried to understand it, the more confused she became. Someone had to know the answers. Why did the file say her room was unoccupied? It was clear that someone put her here in this horrible, godforsaken place. Why would they hide the fact that she was here? What secrets did her past hold that needed to be kept a mystery? She looked at her wrinkled hands. Why did she have no memory of growing this old? What happened during those forgotten years? Had someone given her drugs to erase her memory? The cocoa here had an awful after taste. She always was more disorientated shortly after drinking it. Could there be some ulterior motive for her loss of memory? No one could fall off the face of the earth without someone missing them. Could they? She had to find out somehow before she lost what little sanity she had left.

She heard the dinner bell sound. She returned the handkerchief to its hiding place. She slowly gathered up the strength to walk down to the center hall. It looked like the rest of the residents had arrived there way ahead of her. She found an empty chair at the corner table. The cook came over and plopped a plate of food down in front of her. "Well her majesty finally decided to grace us with her presence." The cook stared down at her. "What is the matter your majesty, isn't the food up to your high faluting standards?"

She bowed her head, "Everything is fine, just fine." She picked up her fork and cut into the meat.

The cook gave one last huff then scurried back to the kitchen.

She brought the fork up to her mouth when she caught the whiff of an unusual odor besides the food. She set the fork back down on the plate. The other residents looked at her, then at her plate. She slid the plate toward them. They glanced around then quickly divided the food between them, then slid the plate back in front of her.

She smiled at them before she rose. She walked over to the large window leaning her head against the smooth cool glass and closed her eyes. Nothing made sense to her. She should be able to remember something about her life. The pictures on the bedroom wall wanted to convey something but she could not understand what they were trying to tell her.

A tear slid down her cheek as she opened her eyes to watch the rain pound on the cement patio. Pools of water flooded the patio. She was about to leave when she saw them. The girl was back and this time a young man was with her. She held her breath as she watched him lift her high above his head, swirling through the rain. Her hands were on his shoulders as she laughed and threw her head back, allowing the rain to drench her face. He slid her down his body until they were eye to eye. He said something before drawing her to his lips. She reciprocated the kiss as she wrapped her arms around him and intertwined her finger in his hair.

She placed her hand on the window as they slowly swirled away in the rain. Her soul cried out to be with the couple. There she would find the answers to all the questions that escape her and the peace that went with them. Why couldn't she remember? She turned to see the dinner dishes had been removed. In their place were board games and the elderly playing cards.

She went over to a chair by a lamp and sat down. She picked up a magazine. The date on the cover stated it was fifty years old. She shook her head and thumbed through it. She stopped and stared at the full page picture. There in the picture was the same girl she saw moments ago dancing with the young man out on the patio. The caption read: Up and coming in the world. She turned the page to another one of the couple embracing in the rain. The story to accompany the pictures was torn out of the magazine. She carefully looked around before tearing the page out, folded it and slipped it in her pocket.

She went over to the computer station for the residents' use. She sat down and pushed the button to turn the ancient computer on. It let out wheezes as the screen flashed to life. She took a deep breath and clicked on the search engine then entered the magazine's name.

Her finger hovered over the enter key. If this worked she could maybe locate the young girl and ask her to help her find out who she was and why she was in this awful place. She finally got up the nerve and clicked enter.

The computer flickered for several minutes as it tried to retrieve the information she sought. The flickering got worse and then the computer went black. She looked up to see a nurse drop the now unplugged cord of the computer on the floor.

The nurse gave her a small smile, "Sorry, you cannot use the computer in a rain storm. There is too much of a chance of being electrocuted from lightning striking the lines outside. Why don't you read or try your hand at a game of Bridge?"

She shook her head in defeat. "That is okay, but I am a little tired, so I may go and rest awhile." She got up and went back to her room.

She opened the door to see the nurse searching her bed for something. The nurse was startled when she appeared before expected. "May I help you find whatever you are looking for?"

The nurse gave a huff as she straightened the bed. "One of the staff is missing an embroidered handkerchief. We are making a search of all the rooms in order to find it for them."

"Well did you find it in here?"

"No, I did not expect to find it here but we had to check all the rooms. Good-night." The nurse made a hasty retreat.

She waited until she could no longer hear the nurse's footsteps before she went over to the chaise and removed the handkerchief from its hiding place. Why were they so interested in this handkerchief? How did they know she might have it? She sat down, and held the handkerchief against her nose. Her nose picked up a faint trace of his essence. It brought a calming peace to her soul. She drank it in as a drowning person would the last drops of oxygen. She closed her eyes trying to remember why his essence was able to have this effect on her. His gentle gray eyes appeared in her mind. They were looking back at her from under the hood of a muscle car. "I will be done in just a little bit then I will cleanup and we can go."

She looked at her reflection in the windshield and the young girl's reflection stared back at her. Her eyes flew open breaking the trance. How could she have seen the young girl's reflection when it should have been the old crone she sees in the mirror every morning? Is the young girl her in an earlier stage of her life? She went to the pictures on the wall again. Yes, the woman could be the young girl. Were these really part of her past or were they of someone she knew?

Her head hurt trying to sort everything out so she went over and lay down on the bed. She closed her eyes and was soon dreaming of the young girl dancing in the rain.

CHAPTER 6

She heard a light rap on the door. The door opened to reveal the elderly man carrying a covered tray. "May I come in?"

"Yes, please do. I have something I wish to discuss with you."

"Alright, we can have a cup of cocoa while we talk." He came in and shut the door.

He came over and set the tray down on the coffee table. He sat beside her as he took off the lid to the delicious aroma of cocoa and petit fours. He poured a rich cream in the bottom of the cups before pouring in the cocoa. He topped off the cup with handful of marshmallows. As he was about to hand her the cup, she interrupted him by handing him the handkerchief. "You did not have to have the nurse look for this. You may have it back. Please explain why this handkerchief is in one of the photographs hanging over on the wall?"

He closed his hand around hers. "I did not ask anyone to find this handkerchief. They must be trying to remove everything from your past. Well sweet thing drink up and have a couple of petit fours." He took a deep draw of cocoa as he turned. "It's good, but not as great as when you make it and the petit fours."

Her lips trembled, "I make these?"

"You used to be a wonderful chef before they brought you here. You kept me well fed."

"You know me? Where are we? Why are we here? Who brought me here? Why did you allow them to take me?" The mug clattered as she set it on the table. "Please help me! I don't know where I am or even who I am. I look at my reflection and a strange old crone stares back at me. Help me get out of here and back to where I belong."

He set his mug down and caressed her check. His touch was soft and comforted her soul. Suddenly she was jarred awake by a clap of thunder. She had been dreaming. She shook her head as tears slid down her face. Would this nightmare never end?

She got up and pulled the handkerchief and magazine page from their hiding place. She smoothed the wrinkles out of the page and studied the picture of the young girl. The picture had been taken at night. The young girl was swinging around a street light. Her white dress billowed with movement as her laughing smile stared back at her.

She traced the outline of the young face then did the same to her own face. She could not distinguish whether or not they had the same shaped face. The joy captured in the photograph beckoned to her to embrace it. But how could she embrace the joy when there was so much missing in her life. How could this young girl appear before her when this photograph was taken at least fifty years ago? She had to be a figment of her imagination. Some lost fragment of memory resurfacing.

Maybe she could have been the one who took the photograph of the young girl and the couple. This made more sense to her than she being the young girl.

She carefully folded them together and slid them through the seam in the couch pillow on the chaise away from prying eyes. She started to turn when she caught a glimpse of the petit four on a small plate sitting on her nightstand by her bed. She ran over and snatched it up. It was real. She could see it, feel it, and she popped it into her mouth. She could taste it. Its delicious favor exploded across her taste buds. She savored it as it melted on her tongue. How could this be a figment? But yet it had to be, there was no other logical explanation for it.

She heard doors banging open and shuffling feet passed her door. She gave a sigh as she got dressed for another dreary day. After breakfast, the sun popped out from behind the dark clouds that were left from last night's storm. She welcomed the sunshine on her face as she sat by the window.

A nurse came by and joined her. "It finally has stopped raining for awhile according to the weather forecaster. Everyone will be able to go out on the patio this afternoon. I know the flowers will enjoy the attention you will give them. They have never bloomed so much. It is all you're doing, that caused their wonderful display. Thank you."

She looked up at the nurse, with questioning eyes. "Oh dear, are you having another one of your spells? Let me get the head nurse."The nurse started to leave. She quickly touched her arm to stop her.

"No, please, I'm fine, just being a little melancholy that's all with all the rain. Yes it will be nice to go out and do some gardening."

The nurse shook her head in understanding as she left to attend to her duties.

CHAPTER 7

The doctor looked down at the notations in the special chart he kept in a separate file cabinet in his office. The head nurse was the only other one with access to these files in his office. The prognosis did not seem too encouraging. She seemed to be slipping farther away from reality. The staff had reported she questioned them about nonexistent staff members and an unexplainable soaked gown was found in her laundry. He reached over and buzzed the intercom. "Please come in here. I have some questions to ask you."

The door opened and the head nurse came in and sat down across from him. She glanced at the file on his desk and shook her head. "I know what you are going to say. Yes, she seems more despondent even after you changed her medication. We had to start putting the medication in her food since we found the stash of pills in her bathroom. Her plate is always clean by the time the meal is over."

"What about her interaction with the rest of the residents? Have there been any incidents? Has the handkerchief been found? We do not want another episode like the last time she had it in her possession." He made a notation in the file.

The head nurse shook her head. "No, she usually sits by the window staring at the rain. She did try to use the computer but we had to unplug it because of the storm with all the lightning."

"Well I will up her dosage another gram per dose and see if that helps. Please keep an extra close eye on her to make sure there are no side effects with the new dosage. We can't have her going off on a drug induced hallucination with her connections. I was hoping after forty years there would be some sort of change in her condition. After all you can only do so much with drugs when a person is her age before the drugs no longer are effective." He closed the file.

The head nurse rose and went to the door. "We will do our best to keep her comfortable." and then left shutting the door behind her. She grumbled all the way back to her desk, "Right, I have nothing better to do with my time than to hold an over the hill celebrity's hand that should have been in an assisted-living ward instead of independent living ward."

CHAPTER 8

She knelt by the flower bed, pruning out the dead headed flowers. She placed them in a bucket for the compost pile then turned to weed out the bed. The weeds went in a pail for the trash. The rain made it easy to pull the weeds from the dirt. She reached way back into the flower bed for a stubborn weed when she saw a small light blue carnation growing amidst the ground cover.

The weed was forgotten as she pulled out her small spade and dug around the fragile plant, careful not to damage its root system. Soon she had the carnation in her hand and over to the potting shed. She planted it in a pot. How had it come to be planted there? She remembered when she planted the whole flower bed. The nursery had run out of carnations. She had been upset which caused her to lose her privilege to work on the flower beds for two weeks. She had to be content to watch the flowers through the window as they took root in the bed.

Now she had to figure out how to get the flower pot past the orderly and to her room. She glanced about as the other residents milled around the patio watching the birds as they fluttered from branch to branch singing to their mates. This gave her an idea. She quickly gathered a couple of small bags of bird seed and handed them to a couple of frail ladies in wheelchairs. She whispered to them to sprinkle the seed around their chair and on their laps so the birds would come to them, when the orderly was not looking.

Sheer delight spread across the ladies faces as they did as she instructed. The birds were more than delighted to join in on the feast spread before them. The orderly turned back around to find the patio and ladies covered with chirping birds wanting more seed. She waited until he was busy trying to shoo the birds away from the residents to take her prize and make a break for her room.

She closed her room door as pandemonium broke out on the patio as the elderly ladies quarreled with the orderly about feeding the birds on their laps. She placed the carnation in front of her window.

She was coming down the hallway when the head nurse stopped her. "I do not know what your reasoning was to cause this pandemonium on the patio but I will not have any more of your shenanigans disrupting this ward. Get back to your room and stay there. I will have your meals delivered to you for the next three days. Maybe then you will behave yourself." The head nurse took her by the arm and gently escorted her back to her room.

She went with the nurse and when the door closed she turned back to the small carnation. She could not believe her eyes. She ran over to the pot. There, growing entwining with each other were two carnations. The small light blue one was twisting around with a blood red carnation.

CHAPTER 9

For two days she watched the carnations grow from mere seedling to mature plants. They mystified her. Carnations do not intertwine nor do they mature so fast. Their fragrance filled her room with their delicate bouquet. She could envision beds of carnations flowing down through the deep yard. Honey bees buzzed happily from flower to flower gathering nectar. Where was this beautiful garden? Why could she envision it so vividly? Peace filled her soul when she thought of it. It was almost as if she could reach out and touch the flowers.

She decided to try. She reached out as far as she could and to her surprise she touched the petals. She knelt down brushing her cheek across the delicate soft petals. They melted the last of her inhibitions. She rose and slowly meandered through the flower beds. In the middle of the yard, she heard faint laughter. She glanced to her left and there the young girl stood fifty yards away. A woven wreath of carnations adorned her head. The girl laughed again and danced off twirling through the flower beds.

She smiled and followed the girl as fast as she could, yet the space between them never shrank. Soon, she heard a deep laugh answering the sweet young purls of laugher. She searched the darken shadows at the far edge of the yard. There he stood waiting for her. His arms opened wide to greet the young girl's embrace. The girl stopped dancing and looked around and saw her. The girl smiled and waved then turned and ran toward the young man.

She ran after the girl crying out for her to wait. The young girl just ran on. The young man ran towards the girl and snatched her up in his arms, twirling them around as their laugher mingled together. He set her down as he took her hand in his then they set out running deeper into the shadows.

She ran faster and faster trying to catch up with

them. It started to rain as she entered the shadows. Tears mingled with the rain as she would catch glimpse of them in the darken shadows. She lost sight of them when she stumbled and fell against the wall of her room. She slid to the floor as tears streamed down her face, "NO, oh please no! Come back! I need you! Please help me!" Outside the thunder rumbled.

CHAPTER 10

The rain beat down on her. Where was she? The last she knew she was in her room by the wall. She reached out her hand and felt the deep pile of wet leaves at her knees. She carefully rose to her feet. Her legs felt like they were made of rubber bands. She tried to wipe the rain from her face so she could see where she was. The rain would not cooperate. It continued to pour down in sheets. It distorted her surroundings. She thought that she was in the midst of a forest but that could not be true, could it?

She stumbled along the tiny path groping her way along. The rain had drenched her to the skin. She now shivered with each step she took. How had she gotten here? Why was she here? What was she looking for? None of this made any sense to her. Something urged her on, making her take another step when all she wanted to do was to lie down and quit. The bark of the trees scratched and gouged at her hands as she tried to stay upright. She stumbled again as a raised root caught the toe of her shoe. She hit her head against the base of the tree ripping a gash across her forehead. Blood now mingled with the flow of rain in her eyes. She cried out in pain as she turned lying on her back. The rain cleared the blood from her eyes.

Why did she want to continue? Every molecule of her body was crying out in agony. Her limbs did not want to respond to her mind's request for movement. Her strength was draining away fast. If she could not move she would die here, alone, no one would know or care what happened to her.

No she would not allow this to be how she died. She groaned as she reached out and grabbed the root of the tree. She pulled herself up into a sitting position. The rain had let up some and she thought she saw glimmers of lights through the trees. She crawled up the base of the tree. Her fingers dug in the bark to help steady her wobbly legs. She held her arm out in front of her to help balance herself as she stepped unsteadily.

She forced her feet to continue through the pain. Each step sent shooting pain through her body. Still she forged ahead one step at a time heading for the twinkling lights. The rain slowed to a drizzle now. The trees thinned out showing the lights were headlights of passing vehicles on a road through the forest. Hope sprang up in her soul. If she could get to the road she could find help. She doubled her effort willing her body forward.

The rain had all but stopped by the time she drug her body out to the edge of the deserted road. She bowed her head resting it on the ground in frustration. She had made it yet fate was again against her. She heard it before she saw the headlights of the muscle car. She crawled up on her knees with great effort. She hoped that it would be enough for them to see her. The lights grew brighter as the car came closer to the curve in the road. As the car started to make the curve there was a tremendous rumbling then the car was hit in the side by a landslide. The car tumbled over the side of the road landing against a large tree.

Oh no, how could this happen? She crawled over to a road sign and pulled herself up. She stumbled over to the landslide most of which was piled against the side of the muscle car. She shook her head trying to clear her mind at what she saw. She knew this car. She had seen it before. It was his car, his muscle car. She had to help him.

She turned as she heard the rumble of a semi coming up the road. She stumbled out into the middle of the road waving her arms franticly. The headlights blinded her as she heard the airbrakes slam on. She held her arm in front of her face as a shield against the glare of lights. She pointed to the car as she heard heavy footsteps running toward her. "Help! Please help them! They are trapped in the car by the landslide."

She sat on the back bumper of the emergency unit wrapped in a blanket. The flashing lights drove the darkness back into the edge of the forest. She listened to the first responders talking to each other as they worked to free the occupants of the car. "The toddler is fine, just a few scratches. The mother has a gash across her forehead. It's the driver that we are going to have trouble with. The door bashed into him as they hit the tree. Somehow he twisted in his seat and received the main blow to his spine. It looked like he was trying to reach the toddler in the backseat."

"Yeah, he will be lucky if he lives through this. The best he can look forward to if he makes it will be a life in a wheelchair."

CHAPTER 11

She woke crumbled against the wall. She stretched her legs trying to get the circulation worked back into the muscles so she could stand. These nightmares were getting too real. She was afraid next time she would not be able to wake from them. Maybe she should talk to the doctor and see if she could get help to stop them. She used the wall to help her to steady her wobbly legs as she made her way to the bathroom. She went to the sink and splashed cool water on her face to clear her mind. She dabbed the water from her face as she glanced up into the mirror.

She dropped the hand towel as she stumbled backwards. It could not be. There was a scar on her forehead that was not there when she last looked in the mirror.

She stumbled out of the bathroom and made it to the chaise before she collapsed. Her mind spun with blinding speed as she tried to make sense of what happened.

The small clock on the small dresser chimed three. She looked at the window. A gentle rain was falling as rain drops raced each other down the window pane.

What is going on? Why could she not remember who she was or why the young girl kept appearing to her? It was as if she was losing what little mind she had left.

There was a soft knock on the door. She called out for whoever was there to come in. The door opened and revealed the elderly man holding a covered tray. He had come back for her. He came over and set the tray on the table then sat down beside her. He caressed her cheek as his gray eyes twinkled bright.

She reached up and encased his hand against her cheek. She closed her eyes as she allowed the heat from his hand to warm her chilled skin. She released his hand expecting him to disappear before her eyes. She felt his finger lift her chin as his lips brushed softly across hers. It almost made she swoon. So much love flowed through the brief touch she thought she could not handle any more. She opened her eyes to his gray eyes. "Do I know you? I feel like I have known you for all my life. But I cannot even remember who I am? All I know is, I want out of here and someone out there will be waiting for me. Can you help me? Do you know where I should go to find out the answers to my unanswerable questions?"

"That is why I'm here. Soon you will be safe and remember everything." He stood and went to the door, listening before he opened it a crack. "Fantastic, the hallway is clear. Let's make sure you stay nice and warm on our trip." He went to the closet and pulled out a crochet wrap and held it out for her.

She pulled out the hidden objects as she rose slowly, hobbling to him. She allowed him to drape the wrap around her shoulders. She glanced over at the carnations. They were drooping and petals were dropping on the table.

He held her hand as they slowly entered the hallway. The long metal hand rails ran along each side on the walls, waist high. Loose, stained, black and white tile creaked under their feet as she followed as fast as the ancient body that held her prisoner would allow. Her legs wobbled severely. He wrapped a strong arm around her, giving her the needed help to continue. They heard voices as they approached the next corridor. He held a finger to his lips then peeked around the corner, viewing two burly men in white leaning against the central desk, talking to the night nurse.

She crept up and seeing them at the desk, the hope that sprang in her heart died. There was no way they could get past them without being seen. The sparkle in his eyes shone brightly in the dim hallway. He looked around the corner at the group. His brow drew down; concentrating sharply, then a door started slamming down the other hallway as screams quickly followed.

All three of the staff hurried down the hallway to quiet things down before the whole ward was awake. He smiled and took her hand guiding her toward the front door as fast as she could travel. Her legs moved faster and were more stable the nearer they came to the door.

She grabbed his sleeve to stop him from setting off the door alarm as he reached for the doorknob. She stared at her hand that held his sleeve. The skin was firm on the thin fingers. Her other hand flew to her mouth to muffle the scream in her throat. He smiled as he removed her hand from his sleeve, bringing it to his lips. She blinked, not believing her eyes; the laugh lines at the corners of his eyes were gone. There was barely any gray in his hair now.

He laughed as he pushed the door open, pulling her through. The alarm screamed, alerting the staff to their escape. "This way, it's not that far sweetheart. We can make it. Trust me." He urged her on.

They slowly ran around the edge of the building into the parking lot. The rain had stopped. Thick gray fog swirled around their ankles. The fog was at their waist by the time they reached the other side of the parking lot. They heard the front door slam against the wall as the orderlies poured out the door, cursing at the subterfuge that had allowed their escape.

They quickened their pace and she found she could easily keep up with him. Her body no longer throbbed as she stretched her legs farther than she could remember with each step she took. Soon, he was no longer leading her. She drew abreast of him. The shawl fluttered away. Their steps fell in unison against the ground. The voices of the orderlies grew fainter as they stretched out their stride. They ran throughout the night and the fog swirled over their heads, now distorting the trees to gray.

She no longer could make out images around them, yet their feet did not stumble. A Byzantium lace dress swung freely on her slim frame. Something drew her forward; her fear was left far behind. Beside him, she felt she could accomplish the greatest task fate threw at her.

The terrain angled up sharply, yet it did not tax her strength. She felt more robust with each step. Her lungs drew in clean pure air, cleansing her soul. The terrain leveled off at the top of the hill. She swirled, laughing as she gave herself a hug over their escape. She twirled allowing the Byzantium lace dress to flare out. She ran her slim hands down the dress. She could not believe she was free from that horrible place. Her soul felt so light as if she could take wing and fly. She turned, and in the place of the elderly man stood the love of her life. His wavy brown hair fell lightly across his forehead as his eyes sparkled bright gray. She danced around him as showers of giggles burst forth from the depths of her soul.

He drew her into his strong embrace; there she felt the love she missed for so long. She leaned up, encircling his neck as he leaned down, drinking passion deep from her lips. When they parted he drew her hand down and kissed her fingers before sliding her wedding ring back on her finger. He swept her up in his arms as the fog parted, the first warm rays of the morning sun peeking over the horizon. She laughed as she hugged him back, drinking in the love flowing from his lips.

CHAPTER 12

The mourners filed slowly by the light blue casket. The sky blue carnations blended with the baby's breath on top of the casket. The red ribbon flowing from the bouquet read Mother and Grandmother. The funeral director came up to the grieving family as the last of the mourners filed out the door. He helped the middle-aged woman up as her children followed them to the casket to pay their last respects.

The middle-aged woman hung her head, dabbing a handkerchief as a new batch of tears formed in her eyes. "I still don't understand how she got clear across the state in one night and found the cemetery in the dark. She could barely walk across the room. We shouldn't have put her in the rest home. I should have kept her with us. I know she fought us about it. She wanted to stay by him.

You would have thought she would have been relieved after Father passed away. She never left his side after the car accident. Even through all the physical therapy, they warned her that he would never leave the wheelchair. But she always told me there was more to love than a pair of legs. Why didn't I listen to her? I thought she ruined her life, giving up her career so she could care for him. If we listened to her, she would still be alive."

The funeral director shook his head in understanding, "The only explanation they could come up with is that someone kidnapped her, drove her there, and left her to die. They found a tray of cocoa and petit fours in her bedroom that night. I'm so sorry this happened when you were so far away from her." The funeral director held her hand as they drew close to the casket.

The woman looked down at her mother lying in the casket. Her mother's hands were folded across her chest, held a sky blue carnation over an embroidered handkerchief. The sunlight streaming through the window shimmered and shined off her wedding ring. The magazine page lay at her head. The smile on her face had not faded over the years. The smile lit up her face, making it seem to glow with contentment.

The woman drew back in horror. One hand flew to her chest as she staggered and grabbed the edge of the coffin for support. Her eyes squeezed shut. She gasped for air that had abandoned her lungs. Her husband quickly slid his arm around her waist for support. She slowly gained her composure. She glared at the funeral director.

She seized her mother's hand, not believing what her eyes saw. "How, how did you get this ring and picture? My mother placed them in my father's hand the day we buried him forty years ago."

ABOUT THE AUTHOR

Sue Raymond was born and raised in the Midwest along with her siblings. Sue was trained in the Commercial Art field before marrying her husband. After raising two sons and having five grandchildren Sue started a new avenue in her life, writing. She has eight published novels as she works on four other novels and children's stories.

Thank you for reading 'Window Pane'. I would like to ask you to please leave an honest comment on one of the sites you found the book about how you liked or did not like it.

You can find my other novels at sueraymondladylaindora.wordpress.com.

Titles:

The Perfect Witness

Hidden Secrets

Rendezvous with the Past

Death Plummet

Blizzard Terror

Resin La Rock

Healer of Surflex by Lady Laindora

Iowa's Original Writers Anthology 2015

Future titles in the works:

Grampa's House Needs Painting

Seeds of Chance

The Muddy Seed

A Sled Ride with Daddy

A Snowy Seed of Love

Healer of Surflex Color book

The Rose Competition

Sudan Terror

Sue Raymond

Window Pane

Sue Raymond

www.ingramcontent.com/pod-product-compliance
Lightning Source LLC
Chambersburg PA
CBHW071012120726
47910CB00004B/1481